SMALL THINGS LIKE THESE

Further praise for *Small Things Like These*:

'An epic distilled down to a single potent essence . . . A finely etched portrait of a society, a glimpse into the heart of darkness that was the Magdalen laundry system, a moving reflection on moral choice and a quietly brilliant artistry.' Fintan O'Toole, *New Statesman* Books of the Year

'I loved *Small Things Like These* . . . Her writing is invariably elegant and sharp at the same time, and she handles Irish social history with oblique precision.' Sarah Moss, *Irish Times* Books of the Year

'Written with precision and rhythmic care . . . a brave and piercing exploration of a most difficult public matter.' Colm Tóibín, *New Statesman* Books of the Year

'A powerful, haunting drama . . . essential reading.' *Sunday Business Post*

'Everything about this remarkable novella feels in some way miraculous . . . The clarity and truth of Keegan's vision never falters. The result is a truly exquisite, tenderly hopeful Christmas tale in which compassion and altruism triumph over apathy and inertia.' *Daily Telegraph*

'A breathtaking tale of the banality of evil and the tangled societal web that sustains it . . . Gripping.' *Sunday Independent*

'This small, exquisite book leaves a large impression . . . Keegan fully exploits the power of understatement . . . Deeply moving.' Damon Galgut, *TLS*

'[Keegan] has an incredible skill of saying so much in just one sentence . . . She wrings so much meaning, atmosphere and feelings from a single cluster of words while keeping the depth. It's sort of witchcraft.' Sara Cox, *The Times*

'The wisest writing is the simplest, and *Small Things Like These* will break your heart with its honesty, steeped in the shock of human kindness. A triumph.' Frank McGuinness

Small Things Like These

CLAIRE KEEGAN

faber

First published in 2021
by Faber & Faber Ltd
The Bindery, 51 Hatton Garden
London ECIN 8HN

This paperback edition first published in 2022

Typeset by Faber & Faber Ltd
Printed in the UK by CPI Group (UK) Ltd, Croydon, CRO 4YY

A CIP record for this book
is available from the British Library

ISBN 978-0-571-36870-9

Printed and bound in the UK on FSC® certified paper in line with our continuing
commitment to ethical business practices, sustainability and the environment.
For further information see faber.co.uk/environmental-policy

This story is dedicated to the women and children who suffered time in Ireland's mother and baby homes and Magdalen laundries.

And for Mary McCay, teacher.

'The Irish Republic is entitled to, and hereby claims, the allegiance of every Irishman and Irish-woman. The Republic guarantees religious and civil liberty, equal rights and equal opportunities to all its citizens, and declares its resolve to pursue the happiness and prosperity of the whole nation and of all its parts, cherishing all of the children of the nation equally.'

Excerpt from 'The Proclamation of the Irish Republic', 1916

1

In October there were yellow trees. Then the clocks went back the hour and the long November winds came in and blew, and stripped the trees bare. In the town of New Ross, chimneys threw out smoke which fell away and drifted off in hairy, drawn-out strings before dispersing along the quays, and soon the River Barrow, dark as stout, swelled up with rain.

The people, for the most part, unhappily endured the weather: shop-keepers and tradesmen, men and women in the post office and the dole queue, the mart, the coffee shop and supermarket, the bingo hall, the pubs and the chipper all commented, in their own ways, on the cold and what rain had fallen, asking what was in it – and could there be something in it – for who could believe that there, again, was another raw-cold day? Children pulled their hoods up before facing out to school, while their mothers, so used now to ducking their heads and running to the clothesline, or hardly daring to hang anything out at all, had little faith in getting so much as a shirt dry before evening. And then the nights came on and the frosts took hold again, and blades of cold slid under doors and cut the knees off those who still knelt to say the rosary.

Down in the yard, Bill Furlong, the coal and timber merchant, rubbed his hands, saying if things carried on as they were, they would soon need a new set of tyres for the lorry.

'She's on the road every hour of the day,' he told his men. 'We could soon be on the rims.'

And it was true: hardly had one customer left the yard before another arrived in, fresh on their heels, or the phone rang – with almost everyone saying they wanted delivery now or soon, that next week wouldn't do.

Furlong sold coal, turf, anthracite, slack and logs. These were ordered by the hundredweight, the half hundredweight or the full tonne or lorry load. He also sold bales of briquettes, kindling and bottled gas. The coal was the dirtiest work and had, in winter, to be collected monthly, off the quays. Two full days it took for the men to collect, carry, sort and weigh it all out, back at the yard. Meanwhile, the Polish and Russian boatmen were a novelty going about town in their fur caps and long, buttoned coats, with hardly a word of English.

During busy times like these, Furlong made most of the deliveries himself, leaving the yard-men to bag up the next orders and cut and split the loads of felled trees the farmers brought in. Through the mornings, the saws and shovels could be heard going hard at it, but when the Angelus bell rang, at noon, the men laid down their tools, washed the black off their hands, and went round to Kehoe's, where they were fed hot dinners with soup, and fish & chips on Fridays.

'The empty sack cannot stand,' Mrs Kehoe liked to say, standing behind her new buffet counter, slicing up the meat and dishing out the veg and mash with her long, metal spoons.

Gladly, the men sat down to thaw out and eat their fill before having a smoke and facing back out into the cold again.

2

Furlong had come from nothing. Less than nothing, some might say. His mother, at the age of sixteen, had fallen pregnant while working as a domestic for Mrs Wilson, the Protestant widow who lived in the big house a few miles outside of town. When his mother's trouble became known, and her people made it clear that they'd have no more to do with her, Mrs Wilson, instead of giving his mother her walking papers, told her she should stay on, and keep her work. On the morning Furlong was born, it was Mrs Wilson who had his mother taken into hospital, and had them brought home. It was the first of April, 1946, and some said the boy would turn out to be a fool.

The main of Furlong's infancy was spent in a Moses basket in Mrs Wilson's kitchen and he was then harnessed into the big pram beside the dresser, just out of reach of the long, blue jugs. His earliest memories were of serving plates, a black range – hot! hot! – and a shining floor of square tiles made of two colours, on which he crawled and later walked and later still learned resembled a draughts board whose pieces either jumped over others or were taken.

As he grew, Mrs Wilson, who had no children of her own, took him under her wing, gave him little jobs and helped him along with his reading. She had a small library and didn't seem to care much for what judgements others passed but carried temperately along with her own life, living off the pension she received on account of her husband having been killed in the War, and what income that came from her small herd of well-minded Herefords, and Cheviot ewes. Ned, the farmhand, lived in too, and seldom was there much friction around the place or with neighbours as the land was well fenced and managed, and no money was owing. Neither was there much tension over religious beliefs which, on both sides, were lukewarm; on Sundays, Mrs Wilson simply changed her dress and shoes, pinned her good hat onto her head and was driven as far as the church by Ned in the Ford, which was then driven a little farther on, with mother and child, to the chapel – and when they returned home, both prayer books and the bible were left lying on the hallstand until the following Sunday or holy day.

As a schoolboy, Furlong had been jeered and called some ugly names; once, he'd come home with the back of his coat covered in spit, but his connection with the big house had given him some leeway, and protection. He had gone on then, to the technical school for a couple of years before winding up at the coal yard, doing much the same work as his own men now did, under him, and had worked his way up. He'd a head for business, was known for getting along, and could be relied upon, as he had developed good, Protestant habits; was given to rising early and had no taste for drink.

Now, he lived in the town with his wife, Eileen, and their five daughters. He'd met Eileen while she was working in the office of Graves & Co. and had courted her in the usual ways, taking her to the cinema and for long walks along the towpath in the evenings. He was attracted to her shiny black hair and slate eyes, her practical, agile mind. When they engaged to marry, Mrs Wilson gave Furlong a few thousand pounds, to start up. Some said she had given him money because it was one of her own that had fathered him – sure hadn't he been christened William, after the kings.

But Furlong never had found out who his father was. His mother had died suddenly, keeled over on the cobblestones one day, wheeling a barrow of crab-apples up to the house, to make jelly. A bleeding to the brain, was what the doctors had called it afterwards. Furlong was twelve at the time. Years later, when he'd gone into the registry office for a copy of his birth certificate, *Unknown* was all that was written in the space where his father's name might have been. The clerk's mouth had bent into an ugly smile handing it out to him, over the counter.

Now, Furlong was disinclined to dwell on the past; his attention was fixed on providing for his girls, who were black-haired like Eileen and fairly complexioned. Already, they were showing promise in the schools. Kathleen, his eldest, came in with him to the little pre-fabricated office on Saturdays and for pocket money helped out with the books, was able to file what had come in during the week and keep an account of most things. Joan, too, had a good head on her shoulders and had recently joined the choir. Both were now attending secondary, at St Margaret's.

The middle child, Sheila, and the second youngest, Grace, who'd been born eleven months apart, could recite the multiplication tables off by heart, do long division and name the counties and rivers of Ireland, which they sometimes traced out and coloured in with markers at the kitchen table. They, too, were musically inclined and were taking accordion lessons up at the convent on Tuesdays, after school.

Loretta, their youngest, although shy of people, was getting gold and silver stars on her copybooks, reading her way through Enid Blyton, and had won a Texaco prize for her drawing of a fat, blue hen skating across a frozen pond.

Sometimes Furlong, seeing the girls going through the small things which needed to be done – genuflecting in the chapel or thanking a shop-keeper for the change – felt a deep, private joy that these children were his own.

'Aren't we the lucky ones?' he remarked to Eileen in bed one night. 'There's many out there badly off.'

'We are, surely.'

'Not that we've much,' he said. 'But, still.'

Eileen's hand slowly pushed a crease out of the bedspread. 'Did something happen?'

It took him a moment to answer. 'Mick Sin-nott's little chap was out on the road again today, foraging for sticks.'

'I suppose you stopped?'

'Wasn't it spilling rain. I pulled over and offered him a lift and gave him what bit of change was loose in my pocket.'

'I dare say.'

'You'd think it was a hundred pound I'd given him.'

'You know some of these bring the hardship on themselves?'

'Tis not the child's doing, surely.'

'Sinnott was stotious at the phone box on Tuesday.'

'The poor man,' Furlong said, 'whatever ails him.'

'Drink is what ails him. If he'd any regard for his children, he'd not be going around like that. He'd pull himself out of it.'

'Maybe the man isn't able.'

'I suppose.' She reached over and sighed, turned out the light. 'Always there's one that has to pull the short straw.'

Some nights, Furlong lay there with Eileen, going over small things like these. Other times, after a day of heavy lifting or being delayed by a puncture and getting soaked out on the road, he'd come home and eat his fill and fall into bed early, then wake in the night sensing Eileen, heavy in sleep, at his side – and there he'd lie with his mind going round in circles, agitating, before finally he'd have to go down and put the kettle on, for tea. He'd stand at the window then with the cup in his hand, looking down at the streets and what he could see of the river, at the little bits and pieces of goings on: stray dogs out foraging for scraps in the bins; chipper bags and empty cans being rolled and blown roughly about by the driving wind and rain; stragglers from the pubs, stumbling home. Some-times these stumbling men sang a little. Other times, Furlong would hear a sharp, hot whistle and laughter, which made him tense. He imagined his girls getting big and growing up, going out into that world of men. Already he'd seen men's eyes following his girls. But some part of his mind was often tense; he could not say why.

It would be the easiest thing in the world to lose everything, Furlong knew. Although he did not venture far, he got around – and many an unfor-tunate he'd seen around town and out the country roads. The dole queues were getting longer and there were men out there who couldn't pay their ESB bills, living in houses no warmer than bunkers, sleeping in their overcoats. Women, on the first Friday of every month, lined up at the post-office wall with shopping bags, waiting to collect their children's allowances. And farther out the country, he'd known cows to be left bawling to be milked because the man who had their care had upped, suddenly, and taken the boat to England. Once, a man from St Mullins got a lift into town to pay his bill, saying that they'd had to sell the Jeep as they couldn't get a wink of sleep knowing what was owing, that the bank was coming down on them. And early one morning, Furlong had seen a young schoolboy drinking the milk out of the cat's bowl behind the priest's house.

While making the rounds, Furlong seldom listened to the radio but he sometimes tuned in and caught the news. It was 1985, and the young people were emigrating, leaving for London and Boston, New York. A new airport had just opened at Knock, in Mayo. The Taoiseach had signed an agreement with Thatcher over The North, and the Unionists in Belfast were out marching with drums, protesting over Dublin having any say in their affairs. The crowds down in Cork and Kerry were thinning out but some still were gathering at the shrines, in the hope that one of the statues might move again.

In New Ross, the shipyard company had closed and Albatros, the big fertiliser factory on the far side of the river, had made several redundancies. Bennett's had let eleven employees go, and Graves & Co., where Eileen had worked, which had been there for as long as anyone could remember, had closed their doors. The auctioneer said business was stone cold, that he might as well be trying to sell ice to the Eskimos. And Miss Kenny, the florist, whose shop was near the coal yard, had boarded up her window; had asked one of Furlong's men to hold the plywood steady for her one evening while she drove the nails.

The times were raw but Furlong felt all the more determined to carry on, to keep his head down and stay on the right side of people, and to keep providing for his girls and see them getting on and completing their education at St Margaret's, the only good school for girls in the town.

3

Christmas was coming. Already, a handsome Norway spruce was put standing in the Square beside the manger whose nativity figures that year had been freshly painted. If some complained over Joseph looking overly colourful in his red and purple robes, the Virgin Mary was met with general approval, kneeling passively in her usual blue and white. The brown donkey, too, looked much the same, standing guard over two sleeping ewes and the crib where, on Christmas Eve, the figure of the infant Jesus would be placed.

The custom was for people to gather there on the first Sunday of December, outside the Town Hall, after dark, to see the lights coming on. The afternoon stayed dry but the cold was bitter, and Eileen made the girls zip up their anoraks and wear gloves. When they reached the centre of town, the pipe band and carol singers had already assembled, and Mrs Kehoe was out with a stall, selling slabs of gingerbread and hot chocolate. Joan, who had gone on ahead, was handing out carol sheets with other members of the choir, while the nuns walked around, supervising and talking to some of the more well-off parents.

It was cold standing around so they walked about the side streets for a while before sheltering in the recessed doorway of Hanrahan's, where Eileen paused to admire a pair of navy, patent shoes and a matching handbag, and to chat with neighbours and others she seldom saw who had come from farther out, taking the opportunity to draw and share what news they carried.

Before long, an announcement was made over the speaker inviting everyone to assemble. The Councillor, wearing his brasses over a Crombie coat, got out of a Mercedes and made a short speech before a switch was flipped, and the lights came on. Magically, then, the streets seemed to change and come alive under the long strands of multi-coloured bulbs which swayed, pleasantly, in the wind above their heads. The crowd made soft little splashes of applause and soon the band piped up – but at the sight of the big, fat Santa coming down the street, Loretta stood back, anxious, and began to cry.

'There's no harm,' Furlong assured. 'Tis just a man like myself, only in costume.'

While other children queued up to visit Santa in the grotto and collect their presents, Loretta stood in tight and held on to Furlong's hand.

'There's no need to go if you don't want, a leanbh,' Furlong told her. 'Stay here with me.'

But it cut him, all the same, to see one of his own so upset by the sight of what other children craved and he could not help but wonder if she'd be brave enough or able for what the world had in store.

That evening, when they got home, Eileen said it was well past time they made the Christmas cake. Good-humouredly, she took down her Odlum's recipe and got Furlong to cream a pound of butter and sugar in the brown delft bowl with the hand mixer while the girls grated lemon rind, weighed and chopped candied peel and cherries, soaked whole almonds in boiled water and slipped them from their skins. For an hour or so they raked through the dried fruit, picking stalks out of sultanas, currants and raisins while Eileen sifted the flour and spice, beat up bantam eggs, and greased and lined the tin, wrapping the outside with two layers of brown paper and tying it, tight, with twine.

Furlong took charge of the Rayburn, putting on tidy little shovelfuls of anthracite and regulating the draught to keep the oven low and steady for the night.

When the mixture was ready, Eileen pushed it into the big square tin with the wooden spoon, smoothing it out on top before giving the base a few hard bangs to get it all into the corners, laughing a little – but no sooner was it in the oven with the door closed than she took stock of the room and told the girls to clear down so she could get on, and start the ironing.

'Why don't ye write your letters to Santa now?'

Always it was the same, Furlong thought; always they carried mechanically on without pause, to the next job at hand. What would life be like, he wondered, if they were given time to think and reflect over things? Might their lives be different or much the same – or would they just lose the run of themselves? Even while he'd been creaming the butter and sugar, his mind was not so much upon the here and now and on this Sunday nearing Christmas with his wife and daughters so much as on tomorrow and who owed what, and how and when he'd deliver what was ordered and what man he'd leave to which task, and how and where he'd collect what was owed – and before tomorrow was coming to an end, he knew his mind would already be working in much the same way, yet again, over the day that was to follow.

Now, he looked at Eileen, unwinding the cord and plugging the iron into the socket, and at his daughters sitting in at the table with their copybooks and pencil-cases to write out their letters – and reluctantly he found himself remembering back to when he was a boy, how he had written away, as best he could, asking for his daddy or else a jigsaw puzzle of a farm in five hundred pieces. On Christmas morning, when he'd gone down to the drawing room Mrs Wilson occasionally let them share, the fire was already lighted and he'd found three parcels under the tree wrapped in the same green paper: a nailbrush and bar of soap were wrapped together in one. The second was a hot water bottle, from Ned. And from Mrs Wilson he'd been given *A Christmas Carol*, an old book with a hard, red cover and no pictures, which smelled of must.

He'd gone outside then, to the cow-house, to hide his disappointment, and cry. Neither Santa nor his father had come. And there was no jigsaw. He thought about the things children said about him in school, the name he was called, and understood this to be the reason. When he'd looked up, the cow, chained to her stall, was pulling hay from the rack, contented. Before going back into the house, he'd washed his face at the horse-trough, breaking the ice on the surface, pushing his hands down deep in the cold and keeping them there, to divert his pain, until he could no longer feel it.

Where was his father now? Sometimes, he caught himself looking at older men, trying to find a physical resemblance, or listening out for some clue in the things people said. Surely some local knew who his father was – everyone had a father – and it didn't seem likely that someone hadn't ever said a word about it in his company for people were bound, he knew, to reveal not only themselves but what they knew, in conversation.

Not long after he'd married, Furlong decided to ask Mrs Wilson if she knew his father but hadn't, on any evening he'd gone out to visit, been able to summon the courage; to her it might have seemed ill-mannered after all she'd done for them. Not more than a year afterwards, Mrs Wilson took a stroke and was taken into hospital. When he had gone in to see her, on the Sunday, she'd lost the use of her left side and was past speech but she recognised him, and lifted her good hand. Like a child she was, sitting up in the bed, gazing out the window, a flowery nightgown buttoned to her chin. It was a blustery afternoon in April; beyond the wide, clear panes, a blizzard of white blossom was being torn and blown off the roused-up cherry trees, and Furlong had opened the pane a little as she had never liked being in a closed room.

'Did Santy ever come to you, Daddy?' Sheila now asked, eerily.

They could be like young witches sometimes, his daughters, with their black hair and sharp eyes. It was easy to understand why women feared men with their physical strength and lust and social powers, but women, with their canny intuitions, were so much deeper: they could predict what was to come long before it came, dream it overnight, and read your mind. He'd had moments, in his marriage, when he'd almost feared Eileen and had envied her mettle, her red-hot instincts.

'Daddy?' Sheila said.

'Santy came, surely,' Furlong said. 'He brought me a jigsaw of a farm one year.'

'A jigsaw? Was that all?'

Furlong swallowed. 'Finish your letter, a leanbh.'

Some small disagreements rose up between the girls that night as they struggled over choosing which presents they should write away for and what might or could be shared among them. Eileen coached on what was enough and what was too much while Furlong was consulted over spellings.

Grace, who was reaching that age, found it queer that the address wasn't longer.

'"Santa Claus, The North Pole". That can't be all?'

'Everyone up there knows where Santa lives,' Kathleen said.

Furlong winked at her.

'How will we know if they get there on time?' Loretta looked up at the butcher's calendar whose last page of December with its changes in the moon was lifting slightly in the draught.

'Your daddy will post them, first thing,' Eileen said. 'Everything for Santa goes by express.'

She had finished with the shirts and blouses and was starting on the pillowcases. Always, she tackled the hardest things first.

'Turn on the telly there so we can get the news,' she said. 'I've a feeling Haughey will snake back in again.'

Eventually, the letters were put in envelopes which were licked along the gummed seals and placed on the mantel for posting. Furlong looked at the framed photographs of Eileen's family up there, of her mother and father and several others belonging to her, and the little ornaments she liked to collect which somehow looked cheap to him, having grown up in a house with finer, plainer things. The fact that those things had not belonged to him didn't ever seem to have mattered, as they were gladly given the use of them.

Although the next day was a school day, the girls that night were allowed to stay up late. Sheila made up a jug of Ribena while Furlong stationed himself at the door of the Rayburn, toasting slabs of soda bread, comically, on the long fork, which the girls buttered and spread with Marmite or lemon curd. When he burned his black but ate it anyway, saying it was his own fault as he hadn't been watching and had kept it too close to the flame, something caught in his throat – as though there might never again be another night like this.

What, now, was touching him on this Sunday

evening? Again, he found himself thinking back to his time out at Wilson's, and reasoned that he'd just had too much time to dwell and had turned sentimental because of all the coloured lights and the music, and the sight of Joan singing with the choir, how she looked like she belonged there, with all the others – and the scent of the lemon which took him back to his mother at Christmastime in that fine, old kitchen; how she used to put what was left of the lemon into one of the blue jugs with sugar to steep and dissolve overnight and had made cloudy lemonade.

Before long, he caught a hold of himself and concluded that nothing ever did happen again; to each was given days and chances which wouldn't come back around. And wasn't it sweet to be where you were and let it remind you of the past for once, despite the upset, instead of always looking on into the mechanics of the days and the trouble ahead, which might never come.

When he looked up, the time was nearing eleven.

Eileen clocked his gaze. 'It's well past time ye girls were in bed,' she said, replacing the iron in a hiss of steam. 'Go on up now and brush your teeth. And not one peep do I want to hear out of ye before morning.'

Furlong rose then and filled the electric kettle to make up their hot water bottles. When it came up to a boil, he filled the first two, pushing the air from each out in a rubbery little wheeze before twisting the caps on tight. As he waited for the kettle to boil up once more, he thought of the hot water bottle Ned had given him all those Christmases ago, and how, despite his disappointment, he'd been comforted by that gift, nightly, for long afterwards; and how, before the next Christmas had come, he'd reached the end of *A Christmas Carol*, for Mrs Wilson had encouraged him to use the big dictionary and to look up the words, saying everyone should have a vocabulary, a word he could not find until he discovered the third letter was not a k. The next year, when he'd won first prize for spelling and was given a wooden pencil-case whose sliding top doubled as a ruler, Mrs Wilson had rubbed the top of his head and praised him, as though he was one of her own. 'You're a credit to yourself,' she'd told him. And for a whole day or more, Furlong had gone around feeling a foot taller, believing, in his heart, that he mattered as much as any other child.

After the girls had gone to bed and the last of the ironing was folded and put away, Eileen turned off the television and took two sherry glasses from the cabinet which she filled with the Bristol Cream she'd bought to make the trifle. She sighed, sitting in at the Rayburn, then took her shoes off and loosened her hair.

'Your day was long,' Furlong said.

'What matter,' she said. 'That much is done. I don't know why I put the cake on the long finger. There wasn't another woman I met there this evening who hadn't hers made.'

'If you don't slow down, you'll meet yourself coming back, Eileen.'

'No more than yourself.'

'At least I've Sundays off.'

'You have them off but do you take them, is the question.'

She glanced at the door at the foot of the stairs and lifted herself, as though she could sense whether or not the girls were sleeping.

'They're down now,' she said. 'Stretch up your hand there, won't you, and we'll see what's in the post.'

Furlong took down the envelopes and together they opened and read over what was there.

'Isn't it nice to see them showing a bit of manners and not asking for the sun and stars?' Eileen said, after a while. 'We must be doing something right.'

''Tis mostly your doing,' Furlong admitted. 'Where am I ever only away all day then home to the table and up to bed and gone again before they rise.'

'You're all right, Bill,' Eileen said. 'We've not a penny owing, and that's down to you.'

'Their spelling has come on rightly – but what about Loretta with her "Deer Santa"?'

It took a while to go over everything and to decide, between them, what should and should not be bought. In the end, they stretched it out to as much as they could afford: a pair of jeans for

Kathleen, who'd been watching the ad for 501s on television; a Queen album for Joan, who'd glued herself to the Live Aid concert that summer and had fallen in love with Freddie Mercury. Sheila had written the shortest letter, asking plainly for Scrabble, providing no alternative. They decided on a spinning globe of the world for Grace, who wasn't sure what she wanted but had written out a long list. Loretta was not in two minds: if Santa would pleese bring Enid Blyton's *Five Go Down to the Sea* or *Five Run Away Together* or both, she was going to leave a big slice of cake out for him and hide another behind the television.

'There now,' Eileen said. 'There's another job near done. I'll take the bus to Waterford in the morning and shop while they're at school.'

'Would you like me to run you down?'

'You know you'll not have time, Bill,' she said. 'Tomorrow's Monday.'

'I suppose.'

She opened the door of the Rayburn, hesitating, for a moment, before dropping the letters in, on the flame.

'They're getting hardy, Eileen.'

'You know we'll blink a few times and they'll be married and gone.'

'Isn't that the way.'

'The years don't slow down any as they pass.'

She checked the temperature gauge on the oven, whose needle had dropped to very low, where she wanted it, and pulled in a bit tighter.

'So have you decided what you're getting me for Christmas?' she brightened.

'Oh, don't worry,' Furlong said. 'I took the hint there this evening with your little gander around by Hanrahan's.'

'Well, it's nice to see you taking notice and thinking ahead.' She looked well pleased. 'What is it you'd like?'

'There's little I need,' Furlong said.

'Would you like new trousers?'

'I don't know that I would,' Furlong said. 'A book, maybe. I might settle in and read a bit over Christmas.'

Eileen took a sip from her glass and threw him a glance. 'What sort of a book?'

'A Walter Macken, maybe. Or *David Copper-field*. I never did get round to reading that one.'

'Right you are.'

'Or a big dictionary, for the house, for the girls.'

He liked the thought of having a dictionary in the house.

'Is there something on your mind, Bill?' Her finger slid over the top of the glass, circling it. 'You were miles away this night.'

Furlong looked away, feeling her instincts at work again, the hot power of her gaze.

'Was it out at Wilson's you were?'

'Ah, I was only thinking back over a few things.'

'I thought as much.'

'Do you not go back over things, Eileen? Or worry? I sometimes wish I had your mind.'

'Worry?' she said. 'I dreamt last night that Kathleen had a tooth rotten and I was pulling it with the pliers. I near fell out of the bed.'

'Ah, everyone has those nights.'

'I suppose,' she said. 'Coming up to Christmas and the expense of it and all.'

'Do you think they're getting on all right, the girls?'

'What do you mean?'

'I don't know,' Furlong said. 'I wondered over Loretta not going in to see Santa there this evening.'

'She's young yet,' Eileen said. 'Give her time. Won't she find her stride.'

'But aren't we all right?'

'Money-wise, do you mean? Didn't we have a good year? I'm still putting something away into the Credit Union every week. We should get the loan and have the new windows in the front before this time next year. I'm sick of the draught.'

'I'm not sure what I mean, Eileen.' Furlong sighed. 'I'm just a bit weary tonight, is all. Pay no heed.'

What was it all for? Furlong wondered. The work and the constant worry. Getting up in the dark and going to the yard, making the deliveries, one after another, the whole day long, then coming home in the dark and trying to wash the black off himself and sitting into a dinner at the table and falling asleep before waking in the dark to meet a version of the same thing, yet again. Might things never change or develop into something else, or new?

Lately, he had begun to wonder what mattered, apart from Eileen and the girls. He was touching forty but didn't feel himself to be getting anywhere or making any kind of headway and could not but sometimes wonder what the days were for.

Out of the blue, he remembered a job he'd done in the mushroom factory one summer when he was off from the technical school. On his first day there, he'd done his best to keep up but had been slow, compared to others, in cutting the line. When he'd reached its end, he was sweating and had paused to look back down the line to the point where he'd started, and saw there the young mushrooms already starting to push through the compost again – and his heart had fallen, knowing the same would happen all over again, day after day, for the whole summer long.

For a minute he endured a strong, foolish need to go over this with Eileen but she perked up and began sharing the news she'd carried from the Square: the middle-aged undertaker people said would never marry had proposed to a young waitress, half his age, who worked at Murphy Flood's

Hotel in Enniscorthy, had taken her into town and bought her the cheapest ring off the tray at Forristal's. The barber's son, a young electrician who was still serving his time, had been diagnosed with some rare type of cancer and was given no more than a year to live. There was a report that several more out at Albatros would be made redundant after Christmas – and people said that the circus might come to town early in the new year, of all times. The postmistress had given birth to triplets, all boys, but that was yesterday's news. She'd heard, too, that the people out at Wilson's had sold off all the livestock and hadn't more than a few dogs about the place, that all the land was leased out and under tillage now, and that Ned had a touch of bronchitis.

When the talk dried up, Eileen reached out for the *Sunday Independent* and gave it a shake. Not for the first time, Furlong felt that he was poor company for her, that he seldom made a long night shorter. Did she ever imagine how her life would be if she had married another? He sat on, not un-happily, listening to the clock ticking on the mantel and the wind piping eerily in the flue. The rain had come on again, was blowing hard against the windowpane and making the curtain move. From inside the cooker, he heard a lump of anthracite collapsing against another, and put a little more on.

At some stage, the need for sleep came over him but he made himself sit on, dozing and waking in the chair, until the hour hand of the clock hit three and a knitting needle, pushed down deep into the heart of the Christmas cake, came out clean.

'Well, the fruit's not fallen anyhow,' Eileen said, pleased, and baptised it with a Baby Power.

4

It was a December of crows. People had never seen the likes of them, gathering in black batches on the outskirts of town then coming in, walking the streets, cocking their heads and perching, impudently, on whatever lookout post that took their fancy, scavenging for what was dead, or diving in mischief for anything that looked edible along the roads before roosting at night in the huge old trees around the convent.

The convent was a powerful-looking place on the hill at the far side of the river with black, wide-open gates and a host of tall, shining windows, facing the town. Year round, the front garden was kept in order with shaved lawns, ornamental shrubs growing neatly in rows, the tall hedges cut square. Sometimes, small outdoor fires were made up there whose strange, greenish smoke carried down over the river and across town or away in the direction of Waterford, depending on how the wind was blowing. The weather had turned dry and colder, and people remarked on what a picture the convent made, how like a Christmas card it almost was with the yews and evergreens dusted in frost and how the birds, for some reason, had not touched a single berry on the holly bushes there; the old gardener himself had said so.

The Good Shepherd nuns, in charge of the convent, ran a training school there for girls, providing them with a basic education. They also ran a laundry business. Little was known about the training school, but the laundry had a good reputation: restaurants and guesthouses, the nursing home and the hospital and all the priests and well-off households sent their washing there. Reports were that everything that was sent in, whether it be a raft of bedlinen or just a dozen handkerchiefs, came back same as new.

There was other talk, too, about the place. Some said that the training school girls, as they were known, weren't students of anything, but girls of low character who spent their days being reformed, doing penance by washing stains out of the dirty linen, that they worked from dawn til night. The local nurse had told that she'd been called out to treat a fifteen-year-old with varicose veins from standing so long at the wash-tubs. Others claimed that it was the nuns themselves who worked their fingers to the bone, knitting Aran jumpers and threading rosary beads for export, that they had hearts of gold and problems with their eyes, and weren't allowed to speak, only to pray, that some were fed no more than bread and butter for half the day but were allowed a hot dinner in the evenings, once their work was done. Others swore the place was no better than a mother-and-baby home where common, unmarried girls went in to be hidden away after they had given birth, saying it was their own people who had put them in there after their illegitimates had been adopted out to rich Americans, or sent off to Australia, that the nuns got good money by placing these babies out foreign, that it was an industry they had going.

But people said lots of things – and a good half

of what was said could not be believed; never was there any shortage of idle minds or gossips about town.

Furlong didn't like to believe any of it but he'd gone, one evening, to the convent with a load well before it was due and, finding no sign of anyone at the front, had walked down past the coal house on the gable end and slid the bolt on a heavy door and pushed through to find a pretty orchard whose trees were heavy with fruit: red and yellow apples, pears. He went on with the intention of robbing a freckled pear but as soon as his boot touched the grass, a flock of wicked geese ran out after him. When he retreated, they stood up on their toes and flapped their wings, stretching their necks out in triumph, and had hissed at him.

He'd carried on to a small, lighted chapel where he found more than a dozen young women and girls, down on their hands and knees with tins of old-fashioned lavender polish and rags, polishing their hearts out in circles on the floor. As soon as they saw him, they looked like they'd been scalded – just over him coming in asking after Sister

Carmel, and was she about? And not one of them with shoes but going around in black socks and some horrid type of grey-coloured shifts. One girl had an ugly stye in her eye, and another's hair had been roughly cut, as though someone blind had taken to it with shears.

It was she who came up to him.

'Mister, won't you help us?'

Furlong felt himself stepping back.

'Just take me as far as the river. That's all you need do.'

She was dead in earnest and the accent was Dublin.

'To the river?'

'Or you could just let me out at the gate.'

'It's not up to me, girl. I can't take you anywhere,' Furlong said, showing her his open, empty hands.

'Take me home with you, then. I'll work til I drop for ya, sir.'

'Haven't I five girls and a wife at home.'

'Well, I've nobody – and all I want to do is drown meself. Can you not even do that fukken much for us?'

Suddenly, she dropped to her knees and started polishing – and Furlong turned to see a nun standing down at the confession box.

'Sister,' Furlong said.

'Can I help you?'

'I was just looking for Sister Carmel.'

'She's gone across to St Margaret's,' she said. 'Maybe I can help you.'

'I've a load of logs and coal for ye, Sister.'

As soon as she realised who he was, she changed. 'Was it you that was out on the lawn, upsetting the geese?'

Furlong, feeling strangely chastised, took his mind off the girl and followed the nun out to the front, where she read over the docket and inspected the load to make sure it matched the order. She left him then, going back in the side while he put the coal and logs in the shed, before coming out through the front door, to pay. He took stock of her while she was counting out the notes; she put him in mind of a strong, spoiled pony who'd for too long been given her own way. The urge to say something about the girl grew but fell away, and in the end he simply wrote out the receipt she asked for, and handed it over.

As soon as he got into the lorry, he pulled the door closed and drove on. Farther on, out the road, he realised he'd missed his turn and was heading in the wrong direction with his boot to the floor, and had to tell himself to settle, and go easy. He kept picturing the girls down on their hands and knees, polishing the floor, and the state they were in. What struck him, too, was the fact that when he was following the nun back from the chapel he'd noticed a padlock on the inside of the door that led from the orchard through to the front, and that the top of the high wall separating the convent from St Margaret's next door was topped with broken glass. And how the nun had locked the front door after her, with the key, just coming out to pay.

A fog was coming down, hovering in long sheets and patches, and there was no space on the winding road to turn, so Furlong took a right onto a by-road, and then, farther along, took another right onto another road, which grew narrower. After he'd taken another turn and passed a hayshed he wasn't sure he hadn't already passed, he met a loose puckaun trailing a short rope, and came across an old man in a waistcoat with a bill-hook, out slashing a crowd of dead thistles on the roadside.

Furlong pulled up and bade the man good evening.

'Would you mind telling me where this road will take me?'

'This road?' The man put down the hook, leant on the handle, and stared in at him. 'This road will take you wherever you want to go, son.'

That night, in bed, Furlong considered going over no part of what he'd witnessed at the convent with Eileen, but when he told her, she sat up rigid and said such things had nothing to do with them, and that there was nothing they could do, and didn't those girls up there need a fire to warm themselves, like everyone? And didn't the nuns always pay what was owing and on time unlike so many who would put everything on the slate until you had to put the squeeze on, and there the trouble would come.

It was a long speech.

'What is it you know?' Furlong asked.

'There's nothing, only what I'm telling you,' she answered. 'And in any case, what do such things have to do with us? Aren't all our girls well, and minded?'

'Our girls?' Furlong said. 'What has any of this to do with ours?'

'Not one thing,' she said. 'What have we to answer for?'

'Well, I didn't think there was anything but listening to you now, I'm not so sure.'

'Where does thinking get us?' she said. 'All thinking does is bring you down.' She was touching the little pearly buttons on her nightdress, agitated. 'If you want to get on in life, there's things you have to ignore, so you can keep on.'

'I'm not disagreeing with you, Eileen.'

'Agree or disagree. You're just soft-hearted, is all. Giving away what change is in your pocket and—'

'What ails you tonight?'

'Nothing, only what you don't realise. Wasn't it far from any hardship that you were reared.'

'Far from what hardship, exactly?'

'Well, there's girls out there that get in trouble, that much you do know.'

The blow was cheap but it was the first he'd heard from her, in all their years together. Something small and hard gathered in his throat then which he tried but felt unable to voice or swallow. In the finish, he could neither swallow it down nor find any words to ease what had come between them.

'I'd no call to say that to you, Bill,' Eileen cooled. 'But if we just mind what we have here and stay on the right side of people and soldier on, none of ours will ever have to endure the likes of what them girls go through. Those were put in there because they hadn't a soul in this world to care for them. All their people did was leave them wild and then, when they got into trouble, they turned their backs. It's only people with no children that can afford to be careless.'

'But what if it was one of ours?' Furlong said.

'This is the very thing I'm saying,' she said, rising again. '*Tis not one of ours.*'

'Isn't it a good job Mrs Wilson didn't share your ideas?' Furlong looked at her. 'Where would my mother have gone? Where would I be now?'

'Weren't Mrs Wilson's cares far from any of ours?' Eileen said. 'Sitting out in that big house with her pension and a farm of land and your mother and Ned working under her. Was she not one of the few women on this earth who could do as she pleased?'

5

On Christmas week, snow was forecast. Knowing the yard would be closed for ten days or so, people panicked and called in their last-minute orders complaining, when they did get through, that they had not been able to get through on the telephone. On top of that, the last shipment of the year was late coming in, and due to be collected off the quay. Furlong left Kathleen, who was off from school, in charge of the office while he made the out-of-town deliveries, collecting as much as he could of what was owed. When he came back, at lunchtime, Kathleen had the next loads organised and the dockets ready so there would be only a small delay while he got a bite to eat before delivering more.

On the Saturday, when he got back from the morning round, Kathleen looked fed up, but they were down now to the last batch of orders. She handed him the dockets, saying a big order had just come in from the convent.

'I'll go on out now and tell them to get this one ready before evening,' Furlong said. 'I'll deliver it myself in the morning.'

'Tomorrow's Sunday, Daddy.'

'What choice have I? We're more than full on Monday – and then it's the half-day on Christmas Eve.'

He didn't bother with lunch, just swallowed a mug of tea with a handful of biscuits, feeling the urgency to get back out, but he paused to warm himself for a minute at the gas heater. The heater on the lorry was giving out, and his legs and feet were cold.

'Are you warm enough in here, Kathleen?'

She was sorting the invoices but seemed at a loss to find a space, to put them down.

'I'm all right, Daddy.'

'You're all right?'

'I'm grand,' she said.

'Have any of these men been giving you guff while I was out?'

'No.'

'If so, you have to tell me.'

'There's nothing like that, Daddy. Honest.'

'Swear to God.'

'I swear to God.'

'What, then?'

She turned away and stiffened with the papers in her hand.

'What's the matter, a leanbh?'

She pushed the copy of the convent order down on the spike.

'I just want to go out with my friends to the shops now before they close and see the lights and try on jeans, but Mammy called down earlier and says I have to go with her to the dentist.'

The next morning, when Furlong woke and lifted the curtain, the sky looked strange and close with a few, dim stars. On the street, a dog was licking something from a tin can, pushing it noisily across the frozen pavement with his nose. Already the crows were out, sidling along and letting out short, hoarse caws and longer, fluent kaaahs as though they found the world more or less objectionable. One stood tearing at a pizza box, holding the cardboard down with his foot and pecking, suspiciously, at what was there before flapping his wings and quickly flying off with a crust in his beak. Dapper, some of the others looked, striding along, inspecting the ground and their surroundings with their wings tucked in, putting Furlong in mind of the young curate who liked to walk about town with his hands behind his back.

Eileen was fast asleep, and for a while he watched over her, feeling the need of her, letting his gaze idle over her bare shoulder, her open, sleeping hands, the soot-black darkness of her hair against the pillowslip. The longing to stay, to reach out and touch her was deep, but he took his shirt and trousers from the chair and dressed in the dark, without her waking.

Before going downstairs, he went in to check on Kathleen, who was sleeping after having a tooth pulled. Beside her, Joan stirred a little and turned over, and let out a sigh. In the far bed, Loretta was wide awake. Furlong didn't so much see as sense her eyes shining, through the gloom.

'Are you all right, pet?' Furlong whispered.

'Yes, Daddy.'

'I've to go out now. I'll not be long.'

'Do you have to go?'

'I'll be back in half an hour, child. Go back to sleep.'

In the kitchen, he didn't bother with the kettle or tea, but simply buttered a cut of bread which he ate from his hand before going on, to the yard.

Outside, the streets were slick with frost, and his boots, on the pavement, sounded unusually loud, it being so early on a Sunday. When he reached the yard gate and found the padlock seized with frost, he felt the strain of being alive and wished he had stayed in bed, but he made himself carry on and crossed to a neighbour's house, whose light was on.

When he knocked, softly, on the door, it wasn't the woman of the house who answered it but a youngish woman in a long nightdress and shawl. Her hair, which was neither brown nor red but the colour of cinnamon, fell almost to her waist, and her feet were bare. Behind her, a gas cooker was throwing rings of flame up under a kettle and sauce-pan, and three small children he recognised were sitting around the table with colouring books and a bag of raisins. The room smelled pleasantly of some-thing familiar which he could not name, or place.

'I'm sorry to bother you,' Furlong said. 'I'm from just across the way and trying to get into the yard but the padlock's froze.'

'Tis no bother,' she said. 'Is it the kettle you're after?'

She sounded like she was from The West.

'Aye,' Furlong said. 'If you don't mind.'

She lifted her hair back over her shoulder, and Furlong saw an impression, which was unintended, of her breast, loose, under the cotton.

'The kettle's on. Here,' she said, reaching for it. 'Won't you take it on with you.'

'Surely you'll want this for your tea.'

'Take it on with you,' she said. 'You know there's no luck to be had in refusing a man water.'

When he'd released the padlock and went back and knocked and softly called and heard her say-ing to come in, and pushed the door, a candle was lighted on the table and she was pouring hot milk over bowls of Weetabix for the children.

He stood for a moment taking in the peace of that plain room, letting a part of his mind turn loose to stray off and imagine what it might be like to live there, in that house, with her as his wife. Of late, he was inclined to imagine another life, elsewhere, and wondered if this was not something in his blood; might his own father not have been one of those who had upped, suddenly, and taken the boat for England? It seemed both proper and at the same time deeply unfair that so much of life was left to chance.

'Did you manage?' she asked, taking the kettle.

'Aye,' Furlong said, feeling the cold of her hand in the exchange. 'Many thanks.'

'Will you take a cup of tea?'

'There's nothing I'd rather,' he said, 'but I have to get on.'

'It won't take but a few minutes to boil it up again.'

'I'm near late as it is but I'll get one of the men to leave over a bag of logs for ye.'

'Ah, there's no need.'

'Happy Christmas,' he said, and turned away.

'And the same to you,' she called out, after him.

As soon as he propped the gates open with the blocks, Furlong came back to himself and to what was next. He felt anxious over the lorry but when he turned the key in the ignition, the engine started and he let out a breath he hadn't realised he'd been holding, and left her running. The evening before, he'd checked the load to make sure it matched the order but now found himself checking it again. He looked at the yard too, to see that it was properly swept, and at the scales to see that nothing had been left there overnight, although he'd done these things, he was sure, before he'd locked up yesterday. There wasn't anything he needed in the prefab, but he opened the door and switched on the light and looked over everything: the stacks of papers, the telephone directories and folders, the delivery dockets and copies of the invoices pierced through the spikes. As he was writing out a note for a bag of logs to be left at the house across the way, the telephone rang. He stood watching it until it rang out then waited for a minute or two to see if it would ring again. When he'd finished writing the note, he backed out, and locked the door.

Driving up to the convent, the reflection of Furlong's headlights crossed the windowpanes and it felt as though he was meeting himself there. Quietly as he could he drove past the front door and reversed down the side, to the coal shed, and turned the engine off. Sleepily, he climbed out and looked over the yews and hedges, the grotto with its statue of Our Lady, whose eyes were downcast as though she was disappointed by the artificial flowers at her feet, and the frost glittering in places where patches of light from the high windows fell.

How still it was up here but why was it not ever peaceful? The day had not yet dawned, and Furlong looked down at the dark shining river whose surface reflected equal parts of the lighted town. So many things had a way of looking finer, when they were not so close. He could not say which he rathered: the sight of town or its reflection on the water. Somewhere, voices were singing 'Adeste Fideles'. Most likely these were the boarders at St Margaret's, next door – but surely those girls had gone home? The day after tomorrow was Christmas Eve. It must have been the girls in the training school. Or was it the nuns themselves, practising before early Mass? For a time he stood listening and looking down at the town, at the smoke starting up from the chimneys and the small, diminishing stars in the sky. One of the brightest fell while he was standing there, leaving a streak like a chalk mark on a board for just a second before it vanished. Another seemed to burn out and slowly fade.

When he let down the tail board and went to open the coal house door, the bolt was stiff with frost, and he had to ask himself if he had not turned into a man consigned to doorways, for did he not spend the best part of his life standing outside of one or another, waiting for them to be opened. As soon as he forced this bolt, he sensed something within but many a dog he'd found in a coal shed with no decent place to lie. He couldn't properly see and was obliged to go back to the lorry, for the torch. When he shone it on what was there, he judged, by what was on the floor, that the girl within had been there for longer than the night.

'Christ,' he said.

The only thing he thought to do was to take his coat off. When he did, and went to put it round her, she cowered.

'There's no harm,' Furlong explained. 'I've just come with the coal, leanbh.'

Tactlessly, he again shone the light across the floor, on what excrements she'd had to make.

'God love you, child,' he said. 'Come away out of this.'

When he managed to get her out, and saw what was before him – a girl just about fit to stand, with her hair roughly cut – the ordinary part of him wished he'd never come near the place.

'You're all right,' he said. 'Lean in on me, won't you.'

The girl didn't seem to want him close but he managed to get her as far as the lorry, where she leant against the warmth of the bonnet and looked down at the lights of town and the river, then far away out, much as he had done, at the sky.

'I'm out now,' she managed to say, after a while.

'Aye.'

Furlong pulled the coat a little way around her. She didn't now seem to mind.

'Is it the night time or the day?'

''Tis the early morning,' Furlong explained. ''Twill soon be light.'

'And that's the Barrow?'

'Aye,' Furlong said. 'There's salmon and a big current running there.'

For a moment he wasn't sure that she wasn't the same girl he'd seen in the chapel that day the geese had hissed at him – but this was a different girl. He shone the torch on her feet, saw the long toenails, black from the coal, then switched it off.

'How did you come to be left in there?'

When she made no reply, he felt something of what she must be feeling and rooted emptily in his mind for something comforting to say. After a time, during which some frozen leaves drifted across the gravel, he took a hold of himself and helped her as far as the front door. If a part of him wondered over what he was doing, he carried on, as was his habit, but found himself bracing as he pressed the bell then flinched when he heard it ringing within.

Before long, the door opened and a young nun looked out.

'Oh!' She let a little cry, and quickly shut it.

The girl at his side said nothing but stood staring at the door, as though she might burn a hole through it with her eyes.

'What's going on here at all?' Furlong said.

When the girl again said nothing he again grasped emptily for something to say.

For a good while they waited there in the cold, on the front step. He could have taken her on then, he knew, and considered taking her to the priest's house or on home with him – but she was such a small, shut-down thing, and once more the ordinary part of him simply wanted to be rid of this and get on home.

Again, he reached out and pressed the bell.

'Won't you ask them about my baby?'

'What?'

'He must be hungry,' she said. 'And who is there to feed him now?'

'You have a child?'

'He's fourteen weeks old. They've taken him from me now but they might let me feed him again, if he's here. I don't know where he is.'

Furlong began thinking freshly over what to do when the Mother Superior, a tall woman he recognised from the chapel but had seldom dealt with, opened the door wide.

'Mister Furlong,' she said, smiling. 'How good you are to come and spare us your time so early on a Sunday morning.'

'Mother,' Furlong said. 'Tis early, I know.'

'I'm just sorry you've had to encounter this,' she said, before turning on the girl. 'Where were you?' she changed. 'We're not long after finding that you weren't in your bed. We were about to call the Gardaí.'

'This girl was locked in your shed all night,' Furlong told her. 'Whatever had her there.'

'God love you, child. Come in and get yourself upstairs and into a hot bath. You'll catch your end.

This poor girl can't tell night from day sometimes. Whatever way we are going to mind her, I don't know.'

The girl stood in a type of trance, and had begun to shake.

'Come on in,' the Mother Superior told him. 'We'll make tea. This is a terrible business.'

'Ah, I'll not,' Furlong stepped back – as though the step could take him back into the time before this.

'You'll come in,' she said. 'I'll not have it other-wise.'

'There's a hurry on me, Mother. I've yet to go home and change for Mass.'

'Then you'll come in until the hurry goes off you. Tis early yet – and more than one Mass is being said today.'

Furlong found himself taking his cap off and following, as he was bid, helping the girl along the hall and on through to the back kitchen where a pair of girls were skinning turnips and washing heads of cabbages at a sink. The young nun who'd answered the door was standing at a huge black range, stirring something, and had a kettle on the boil. The whole place and everything in it was shining, immaculate: in some of the hanging pots Furlong glimpsed a version of himself, passing.

The Mother did not pause but carried on, along a corridor of tiles.

'This way.'

'We're making tracks on your floor, Mother,' Furlong heard himself say.

'No matter,' she said. 'Where's there's muck, there's luck.'

She led them on to a fine, big room where a freshly lighted fire was burning in a cast-iron fireplace. A long table, covered in a snow-white cloth, stood surrounded by chairs, and there was a mahogany sideboard, glassed-in bookcases. Hanging over the mantelpiece was a picture of John Paul II.

'Sit in at the fire there now and warm yourself, won't you?' she said, handing him his coat. 'I'll take care of this girl, and see about our tea.'

She went on, closing the door behind her, but hardly had she gone before the young nun came in, with a tray. Her hands weren't steady, and a spoon fell.

'Ye must expect a visitor,' Furlong said.

'Another visitor?' She looked alarmed.

'Tis only a saying,' Furlong explained, 'over when a spoon drops.'

'I see,' she said, and looked at him.

She carried on then, as well as she could, putting out the cups and saucers but struggled in taking the lid off a tin before lifting out a wedge of fruit cake which she sliced up quickly, with a knife.

When the Mother Superior returned, she came slowly to the hearth, where she lifted the tongs and stoked the young fire, pushing the lighted sods skilfully together and surrounding them with fresh lumps of Furlong's best coal, from the scuttle, before seating herself on the armchair opposite.

'So, is all well at home, Billy?' she began.

Her eyes were neither blue nor grey but somewhere in between.

'All's well with us, thank you, Mother.'

'And your girls? How are they? I hear that two of yours are making some progress with their music lessons here. And don't you have another two next door.'

'They're getting on rightly, thank God.'

'And we see another of yours in the choir now. She doesn't look out of place.'

'They carry themselves well.'

'Won't they all soon find themselves next door, in time to come, God willing.'

'God willing, Mother.'

'It's just that there's so many nowadays. It's no easy task to find a place for everyone.'

'I'm sure.'

'Is it five you have, or six?'

'It's five we have, Mother.'

She got up then and took the lid off the teapot, and stirred the leaves. 'But it must be disappointing, all the same.'

Her back was to him.

'Disappointing?' Furlong said. 'In what way?'

'To have no boy to carry on the name.'

She meant business but Furlong, who'd long experience of such talk, was on known ground. He stretched a little and let his boot touch the brass, polished fender.

'Sure, didn't I take my own mother's name,

Mother. And never any harm did it do me.'

'Is that so?'

'What have I against girls?' he went on. 'My own mother was a girl, once. And I dare say the same must be true of you and all belonging to us.'

There was a pause then, and Furlong felt she was not so much put off as changing tack – when the door opened and the girl from the shed was brought in wearing a blouse, cardigan and a pleated skirt and in shoes, with her wet hair badly combed out.

'That was quick.' Furlong half rose. 'Are you any better now, child?'

'Sit in here now, won't you.' The Mother pulled out a chair for her. 'Take some tea and cake and warm yourself.' Gladly she seemed to lift the pot and pour the tea for her, to push the jug and sugar-bowl closer, within the girl's reach.

The girl sat in at the table and awkwardly began picking bits of fruit out of the cake then went about swallowing down the rest with the hot tea, but she struggled over the cup, trying to replace it on the saucer.

For a while, the Mother Superior chatted idly about the news and more unimportant things, before she turned:

'Won't you tell us now why you were in the coal shed?' she said. 'All you need do is tell us. You're not in any trouble.'

The girl froze in the chair.

'Who put you in there?'

The girl's frightened gaze went all around, touched Furlong's briefly before falling back to the table and the crumbs on her plate.

'They hid me, Mother.'

'Hid you how?'

'Weren't we only playing.'

'Playing? Playing what, would you like to tell us?'

'Just playing, Mother.'

'Hide and seek, I dare say. And at your age. Did they not think to let you out when the game was over?'

The girl looked away and let out an unearthly type of sob.

'What ails you now, child? Wasn't it all just a mistake? Wasn't it all just a big nothing?'

'Yes, Mother.'

'What was it?'

'It was a big nothing, Mother.'

'You've had a fright, is all. What you need now is your breakfast and a good, long sleep.'

She looked to the young nun who'd all the while been standing like a statue in the room, and nodded.

'Won't you fry up something for this girl? Take her into the kitchen there and let her eat her fill. And see that she's left idle for today.'

Furlong watched the girl being taken away and soon understood that this woman wanted him gone – but the urge to go was being replaced now by a type of contrariness to stay on, and to hold his ground. Already, it was growing light outside. Soon, the bells for first Mass would ring. He sat on, encouraged by this queer, new power. He was, after all, a man amongst women here.

He looked at the woman before him, at how she was dressed: the well-pressed costume, the polished shoes.

'Didn't Christmas come in quick, in the end,' he idled.

'It did, surely.'

He had to hand it to her; her head was cool.

'You've heard that they're forecasting snow.'

'We could have a white Christmas yet – but isn't it all the more business for you.'

'We're kept busy,' Furlong said. 'I'll not complain.'

'Are you done with this tea or will I pour you another?'

'We may as well finish it, Mother,' he persisted, holding out the cup.

The hand that poured was steady.

'Were your sailors in town this week?'

'They're not my sailors but we had a load come in on the quay there, aye.'

'You don't mind bringing the foreigners in.'

'Hasn't everyone to be born somewhere,' Furlong said. 'Sure wasn't Jesus was born in Bethlehem.'

'I'd hardly compare Our Lord to those fellows.'

She'd had more than enough now, and put her hand down deep, into a pocket, and drew out an envelope. 'I'll expect an invoice for what's owing but here's something for Christmas.'

Reluctant as he was to take it, Furlong stretched out his hand.

She escorted him as far as the kitchen then, where the young nun stood over a frying pan, breaking a duck egg in beside two rounds of black pudding. The girl from the coal shed was sitting in a type of daze at the table, with nothing before her.

They had expected him to go on, Furlong knew, but he paused, contrarily, and stood by the girl.

'Is there anything I can do for you, a leanbh?' he asked. 'All you need do is tell me.'

She looked at the window and took a breath and began to cry, the way those unused to any type of kindness do when it's at first or after a long time again encountered.

'Won't you tell me your name?'

She glanced back at the nun. 'I go by Enda in here.'

'Enda?' Furlong said. 'Is that not a boy's name?'

She wasn't fit to reply.

'But what's your own name?' Furlong gentled.

'Sarah,' she said. 'Sarah Redmond.'

'Sarah,' he said. 'That was my own mother's name. And where do you come from?'

'My people are from out beyond Clonegal.'

'Isn't that well out past Kildavin,' he said. 'How did you come to be here?'

The nun at the cooker coughed and gave the frying pan a rough shake and Furlong understood that the girl could say no more.

'Well, you're upset now, and no wonder. But Bill Furlong is my name and I work at the coal yard, near the quays. If ever there's anything, all you need do is come down or send for me. I'm there every day but Sundays.'

The nun was plating up the egg and pudding, scraping margarine from a big tub, noisily, across a cut of toast.

Deciding to say no more, Furlong went on out and pulled the door closed, then stood on the front step until he heard someone inside, turning the key.

6

'You've missed first Mass,' Eileen said, when he got home.

'Wasn't I up at the convent and then they wouldn't let me leave without going in for tea.'

'Well, it's Christmas,' Eileen said. 'Wasn't it the proper thing to do.'

Furlong made no answer.

'What did they give you?'

'Tea,' he said. 'And cake, was all.'

'But did they not give you something else?'

'What do you mean?'

'For Christmas, I mean. They never let the year pass without sending down something.'

Furlong hadn't thought more of the envelope.

When Eileen opened it and took out the card, a fifty-pound note fell into her lap.

'Aren't they very good,' she said. 'This'll more than pay for what's owing at the butcher's. I'll collect the turkey and ham in the morning.'

'Show me.'

The card depicted a blue sky with an angel and the Virgin and child on a donkey, being led along by Joseph. *The Flight into Egypt*, he read, on the back. On the inside, in a hurried-looking hand, was written: *For Eileen, Bill and Daughters. Many happy returns to you and yours.*

'I hope you thanked them,' Eileen said.

'Why wouldn't I?' Furlong twisted up the envelope and threw it in the scuttle.

'What has you out of sorts?' She was taking the card, putting it up on the mantelpiece beside her other things.

'Nothing,' Furlong said. 'Why?'

'Well, get out of those clothes then and change – or else you'll have us late for second Mass.'

Furlong went out to the back toilet then and took up the soap and lathered his hands slowly at the basin and washed his face and began to shave, drawing the blade very close in places, and nicked his throat. In the mirror, he looked at his eyes, the parting in his hair and at his eyebrows, which seemed to have grown more closely together since last he'd looked at himself. Best as he could he scrubbed his nails, trying to get the black out from under them. With a fresh type of reluctance he then changed into his Sunday clothes and walked with Eileen and the girls to the chapel, feeling the pavement steep and very slippery in places.

'Have ye change for the collection box?' Eileen asked the girls, smiling, as they were entering the chapel grounds. 'Or has your daddy given it all away?'

'There's no need for that type of ugly talk,' Furlong sharpened. 'Have you not enough in your purse for the one day?'

Eileen's smile vanished and a type of astonishment spread across her face. Slowly, she drew out her purse and handed ten-pence pieces round, to the girls.

In the porch, they blessed themselves at the marble font, dipping their fingers in, making ripples on the surface of the water, before going on in through the double doors. Furlong stood down near the door as they walked up the aisle, and watched how easily they genuflected and slid into the pew, as they'd been taught, while Joan carried on up to the front, genuflecting and kneeling there where the choir was seated.

Some women with headscarves were saying the rosary under their breath, their thumbs worrying through the beads. Members of big farming families and business people passed by in wool and tweed, wafts of soap and perfume, striding up to the front and letting down the hinges of the kneelers. Older men slipped in, taking their caps off and making the sign of the cross, deftly, with a finger. A young, freshly married man walked red-faced to sit with his new wife in the middle of the chapel. Gossipers stayed down on the edge of the aisle to get a good gawk, watching for a new jacket or haircut, a limp, anything out of the ordinary. When Doherty the vet passed by with his arm in a sling, there was some elbowing and whispers then more when the postmistress who'd had the triplets passed by wearing a green, velvet hat. Small children were given keys to play with, to amuse themselves, and soothers. A baby was taken out, sobbing in heaves, struggling to get loose from his mother's hold. Cigarette smoke and some bits of laughter drifted in through the porch from out-side, where some of the men always stayed until they heard the starting bell.

Before long, Sister Carmel, who taught the music lessons, sat in before the organ, and began to play. Everyone but the very elderly and handi-capped rose while the altar boys came out, leading the parish priest, whose purple robes swung out behind him, at his heels.

Slowly, he genuflected with his back to the congregation before taking his place at the altar. Opening his arms out wide, he began:

'In the name of the Father and of the Son and of the Holy Spirit. The grace of our Lord, Jesus Christ, and the love of God and the fellowship of the Holy Spirit be with you all.'

'And also with you,' the congregation echoed.

The Mass, that day, felt long. Furlong didn't join in so much as listen, distractedly, while watching the morning light falling through the stained-glass windows. During the sermon, his gaze followed the Stations of the Cross: Jesus taking up his cross and falling, meeting his mother, the women of Jerusalem, falling twice more before being stripped of his garments, being nailed to the cross and dying, being laid in the tomb. When the consecration was over and it came time to go up and receive Communion, Furlong stayed contrarily where he was, with his back against the wall.

Later that Sunday, after they had come home and eaten lamb chops with cauliflower and onion sauce, Furlong put up the Christmas tree then sat at the Rayburn and watched as the girls strung lights, hung decorations and arranged berried holly behind the picture-frames and over the dresser. Feeling not unlike an old man, he rethreaded the small ornaments the girls handed him whose strings had been broken. When the tree was fully decorated and the lights were plugged in and came on, Grace took up the accordion and tried to play 'Jingle Bells'. Sheila turned on the television and lay on the settee watching an episode of *All Creatures*

Great and Small. Furlong wished Eileen would sit down but as soon as she'd washed up she took out the flour and the delft bowl and said they should make the mince pies, and ice the cake. Kathleen made pastry and rolled it out. Then Loretta cut out the rounds with an upturned tumbler while Eileen and Joan separated eggs and beat up the whites and sieved icing sugar. The Christmas cake, already covered in marzipan, was then lifted out and placed on a silver board, and Sheila took up an argument with Grace over the accordion, saying it was her turn to play.

Furlong got up and refilled the scuttle with anthracite from the shed and brought in logs, then took up the brush and began sweeping the floor.

'Do you have to do that now?' Eileen said. 'We're trying to ice the cake.'

When he threw what dust and dirt and holly leaves and bits of pine he'd gathered off the floor into the Rayburn, it spat and let out an almighty crack. It felt as though the room was closing in; the wallpaper with its repetitive, nonsensical pattern was coming before his eyes. A longing to get away came over him and he imagined himself being out in his old clothes on his own, walking the length of a dark field.

By six o'clock, when the Angelus came on the television, followed by the news, several dozen mince pies were cooling on wire racks and the Christmas cake was frosted over, with a little plastic Santa standing almost knee-deep in icing, surrounded by reindeer. When he heard the forecast and looked out and saw the streetlights, Furlong could not sit for longer.

'I might call out to see Ned,' he said. 'If I don't go now, there won't be time to call.'

'Is that what's ailing you?'

'There's nothing ailing me, Eileen.' Furlong sighed. 'Did you not say that the man wasn't well?'

'Then take him these,' she said, wrapping up six mince pies in brown paper. 'And tell him to call in over Christmas.'

'I will of course.'

'He's welcome to come for his dinner on the day, if it suits him.'

'You wouldn't mind?'

'Sure haven't we a house full? What's one more?'

With a type of relief, Furlong put on his over-coat and walked down to the yard. How sweet it felt to be out, to see the river, and his breath on the air. At the quay, a flock of huge, bright gulls floated in and skippered along past him, probably to forage, futilely, at the closed-down shipyard. A part of him wished it was a Monday morning, that he could just put his head down and drive on out the roads and lose himself in the mechanics of the ordinary, working week. Sundays could feel very threadbare, and raw. Why could he not relax and enjoy them like other men who took a pint or two after Mass before falling asleep at the fire with the newspaper, having eaten a plate of dinner?

One Sunday, years ago, while Mrs Wilson was still living, Furlong had gone out to the house. He was not too long married at the time – Kathleen was still in the pram. It was Furlong's habit, on fine Sundays, to get on the bicycle after dinner and go for a visit. As it turned out, Mrs Wilson was not at home that afternoon but Ned was in the kitchen with a bottle of stout, having a smoke at the fire.

He gave Furlong a welcome, as always, and soon began to reminisce over him being brought as an infant into the house, going over how Mrs Wilson used to come down daily to look in at him, in the basket. 'She never once regretted it,' he said, 'or said a cheap word about ye or took advantage of your mother. The wage was small but hadn't we a decent roof over our heads here, and never once did we go to bed hungry. I've nothing only a small room here but never did I go into it to find so much as a matchbox out of place. The room I live in is as good as what I'd own – and can't I get up in the middle of the night and eat my fill, if I care to. And how many can say that?

'But I did a horrid thing, one time. More than once, too, I did it. You were only toddling around back then but there was another man here in those days, milking alongside me in the mornings, and he had an ass and the ass was going hungry for want of grass so he asked me if I'd meet him at the foot of the back lane, at dark, and bring him a bag of hay. It was a hard winter, one of the worst we'd known, and I said I would, and every evening I filled a sack with hay and met him there, near the foot of the lane, where the rhododendrons are, at dark. For a good long while this went on but one night as I was going down the lane, something that wasn't human, an ugly thing with no hands came out of the ditch, and blocked me – and that put an end to me stealing Mrs Wilson's hay. It's too sorry I am now over it, and never once did I tell it to a soul before this only in the confession box.'

Furlong stayed on late that night and drank two small bottles of stout and wound up asking Ned if he knew who his father was. Ned told him that his mother never did say but that many a visitor had come to the house that summer before Furlong was born; big relations of the Wilsons and friends of theirs, over from England, fine-looking people. They used to hire a boat and go fishing for salmon on the Barrow. So who knew whose arms his mother had fallen into?

'God only knows,' he'd said. 'But didn't it turn out all right in the end? Didn't you have a decent start here, and aren't you getting on rightly.'

Before Furlong left, Ned made tea then took up the concertina and played a few tunes before he set the concertina down and closed his eyes and sang 'The Croppy Boy'. The song and the way he sang it made the hairs stand up on the back of Furlong's neck and he wasn't able to leave without asking Ned if he would sing it again.

Now, driving up the avenue, the old oaks and lime trees looked stark and tall. Something in Furlong's heart caught and turned over when the headlights crossed the rooks and the nests they'd built and he saw the house freshly painted, with electric lights burning in all the front rooms, and the Christmas tree on display in the drawing room window, where it never used to be.

Slowly, he drove round the back and parked up in the yard, and turned the engine off. A part of him felt disinclined to go near the house or to make any conversation but he made himself get out and cross the cobblestones, and knocked on the back door. He stood for a minute or two listening before he knocked again – then a dog barked, and the yard light came on. When a woman opened the door and greeted him in a strong, Enniscorthy accent and Furlong explained that he'd come to visit Ned, she told him that Ned was no longer there, that he'd gone into hospital more than a fortnight back, after catching pneumonia, and was now convalescing, in a home.

'Whereabouts?'

'I don't rightly know,' she said. 'Would you like to speak to the Wilsons? They've not sat down to their supper yet.'

'Ah, no. I'll not disturb them,' Furlong said. 'I'll leave it so.'

'Easy knowing you're related.'

'What?'

'I can handy see the likeness,' she said. 'Is Ned an uncle of yours?'

Furlong, unable to find a reply, shook his head and looked past her into the kitchen whose floor was now covered over with lino. He looked at the dresser, too, which was much the same as it had always been with its blue jugs and serving plates.

'Are you sure you wouldn't like me to let them know that you're here?' she said. 'I'm sure they wouldn't mind.'

He could feel her bristling over the door being left open, his letting in the cold.

'Ah, I'll not,' he said. 'I'll head on, but thanks anyhow. Won't you tell them that Bill Furlong called, and wish them a happy Christmas?'

'I will, of course,' she said. 'Many happy returns.'

'Many happy returns.'

When she closed the door, Furlong looked at the worn, granite step and drew the sole of his shoe gratingly across it before turning to see what he could of the yard: the stables and the haybarn, the cow-house, the horse-trough, the wrought-iron gate leading to the orchard where he used to play, the steps to the granary loft, the cobblestones where his mother had fallen, and met her end.

Before he got back into the lorry and pulled the door closed, the yard light went off and a type of emptiness came over him. For a while he sat watching the wind blowing through the tops of the bare trees, the flinching branches, taller than the chimney pots, then he reached out and ate a mince pie from the brown paper. For a good half hour or more he must have sat there, going over

what the woman inside had said, about the likeness, letting it stoke his mind. It took a stranger to
come out with things.

At some point later, an upstairs curtain moved,
and a child looked out. He made himself reach
for the key, and started the engine. Driving back
out the road, he pushed his fresh concerns aside
and thought back over the girl at the convent.
What most tormented him was not so much how
she'd been left in the coal shed or the stance of
the Mother Superior; the worst was how the girl
had been handled while he was present and how
he'd allowed that and had not asked about her
baby – the one thing she had asked him to do
– and how he had taken the money and left her
there at the table with nothing before her and the
breast milk leaking under the little cardigan and
staining her blouse, and how he'd gone on, like a
hypocrite, to Mass.

7

On Christmas Eve, Furlong never felt more like not going in. For days, something hard had been gathering on his chest but he dressed, as usual, and drank a hot Beechams Powder before walking on down, to the yard. The men were already there, standing outside the gates, blowing on their hands and stamping their feet in the cold, chatting amongst themselves. Every man he'd ever kept on had turned out to be decent and wasn't inclined to lean on the shovels or to complain. To get the best out of people, you must always treat them well, Mrs Wilson used to say. He was glad, now, that he always took his girls to both graveyards over Christmas, to lay a wreath against her headstone as well as his mother's, that he'd taught them that much.

After Furlong bade the men good morning and opened the gates, he mechanically checked the yard, the loads and dockets, before getting in behind the wheel. When he started the lorry, a black smoke came from the exhaust. Driving out the road, she laboured on the hills and Furlong knew the engine was giving out, that the new windows Eileen had her heart set upon for the front of the house would not be installed next year, or the year after.

In some of the houses, out the country, it was clear that people were struggling; at least six or seven times he was drawn to one side, quietly, to be asked if what was owing could be put on the slate. At other houses, he did his best to join into the small, festive splashes of conversation and thanked people for their cards, their gifts: tins of Emerald sweets and Quality Street, a sack of parsnips, cooking apples, a bottle of Bristol Cream, Black Tower, a girl's corduroy jacket which hadn't been worn. One Protestant man pressed a five-pound note into his hand and wished him a happy Christmas, saying his son's wife had just given birth to another boy. In more than one house, children, off from school, ran out to greet him, as though he was Santa Claus, just bringing the bag of coal. More than a few times, Furlong stopped to leave a bag of logs at the doors of those who had given him the business, when they could afford it. In one of these, a little boy ran out to the lorry and picked up a lump of coal but his big sister came out and slapped him, telling him to put it down, that it was dirty.

'Fuck,' the boy said. 'Fuck off, why don't you.'

The girl, unashamed, handed Furlong a Christmas card.

'We knew you'd come,' she said, 'and save us having to post it. Mammy always said you were a gentleman.'

People could be good, Furlong reminded himself, as he drove back to town; it was a matter of learning how to manage and balance the give-and-take in a way that let you get on with others as well as your own. But as soon as the thought came to him, he knew the thought itself was privileged and wondered why he hadn't given the sweets and other things he'd been gifted at some of the houses to the less well-off he had met in others. Always, Christmas brought out the best and the worst in people.

When he got back to the yard, the Angelus bell had long since rung but the men were in good spirits and still clearing down, sweeping and hosing off the concrete, joking amongst themselves. Furlong took stock of what was there, marking it all down in the book, then locked the prefab and covered the bonnet of the lorry with sacks in case they got the weather people were expecting. They took turns then, washing at the tap, scrubbing their hands, rinsing the black off their boots. In the finish, Furlong took his overcoat from the lorry and padlocked the gates.

The dinners they ate in Kehoe's that day were paid for by the yard. Mrs Kehoe, wearing a new, festive apron, went around the tables offering more gravy and extra mash, sherry trifle, Christmas pudding and cream. The men ate at their leisure and stayed on, sitting back with pints of stout and ale, passing out cigarettes and using the little red paper napkins she'd left out to blow their noses. Furlong didn't wish to linger; all he wanted, now, was to get home, but he stayed on as it felt proper to idle there for a while, to thank and wish his men well, to spend time on what he seldom made the time for. Already, they had been given their Christmas bonuses. Before he went to settle the bill, they shook hands.

'You must be worn out,' Mrs Kehoe said, when he went up to pay. 'At it all day, every day.'

'No more than yourself, Mrs Kehoe.'

'Heavy is the head that wears the crown.' She laughed.

She was reconstituting leftovers, emptying gravy from the little steel boats into a saucepan and scraping out the mash.

'It's been a busy time,' Furlong said. 'Won't the few days off do us no harm.'

'What it is to be a man,' she said, 'and to have days off.' She gave another, harsher laugh and wiped her hands on her apron before putting the sale through the till.

When Furlong handed her the notes, she put them in the drawer then came out from behind the counter with the change and stood in close, turning her back on the tables.

'You'll put me right if I'm wrong, I know, Bill –

but did I hear you had a run-in with herself above at the convent?'

Furlong's hand tightened round the change and his gaze dropped to the skirting board, following it along the base of the wall, as far as the corner.

'I wouldn't call it a run-in but I had a morning up there, aye.'

''Tis no affair of mine, you understand, but you know you'd want to watch over what you'd say about what's there? Keep the enemy close, the bad dog with you and the good dog will not bite. You know yourself.'

He looked down at the pattern of black, interlocking rings on the brown carpet.

'Take no offence, Bill,' she said, touching his sleeve. ''Tis no business of mine, as I've said, but surely you must know these nuns have a finger in every pie.'

He stood back then and faced her. 'Surely they've only as much power as we give them, Mrs Kehoe?'

'I wouldn't be too sure.' She paused then and looked at him the way hugely practical women sometimes looked at men, as though they weren't men at all but foolish boys. More than once, maybe more than several times, Eileen had done the same.

'Don't mind me,' she said, 'but you've worked hard, the same as myself, to get to where you are now. You've reared a fine family of girls – and you know there's nothing only a wall separating that place from St Margaret's.'

Furlong took no offence, softened. 'I do know, Mrs Kehoe.'

'Can't I count on one hand the number of girls from around here that ever got on well who didn't walk those halls,' she said, splaying her palm.

'I'm sure that's fact.'

'They belong to different orders,' she went on, 'but believe you me, they're all the one. You can't side against one without damaging your chances with the other.'

'Thank you, Mrs Kehoe. I'm much obliged to you for saying.'

'Happy Christmas, Bill.'

'Many happy returns,' Furlong said, pressing the change she'd given him back into her hand.

When he went out, it was snowing. White flakes were coming down out of the sky and landing on the town and all around. He stood looking down at his trousers, the toes of his boots, then screwed his cap down tight on his head and buttoned up his coat. For a while, he simply walked along the quayside with his hands deep in his pockets, thinking over what he'd been told and watching the river flowing darkly along, drinking the snow. He felt a bit freer now, being out in the open air, with nothing else pressing for the time being and another year's work done, behind him, at his back. The urgency to run the one errand he had to run and get on home was falling away. Almost light-heartedly he turned under the lights of town, the long, zig-zagging strands of multi-coloured bulbs. Music was coming from a speaker and a boy's tall, unbroken voice was singing: *O holy night, the stars are brightly shining*. Passing the tree outside the Town Hall, he caught his toe on a paving stone and almost tripped and found himself blaming Mrs Kehoe, who'd made him take a hot whiskey, for his cold, and had given him a huge bowl of sherry trifle. Here and there, he stopped to look into shop fronts, at the merchandise, the snaking lengths of tinsel, so many shining things: Waterford Crystal, sets of stainless-steel cutlery, china tea sets, bottles of perfume, christening mugs. At Forristal's, his gaze rested on black velvet trays stabbed through to display engagement rings and wedding bands, gold and silver watches. Bracelets draped from a false arm – and there were lockets on chains, necklaces.

At Stafford's old shop, he stared as a child might at a hurley stick and sliotar, nets of glass marbles, toy soldiers, plasticine, Lego, draughts and chess sets, at some things which had lasted. Two dolls in frilly dresses sat stiffly with their arms out, their fingers almost touching the pane, as though they were asking to be lifted. When he went in and asked Mrs Stafford if she had a jigsaw of a farm in five hundred pieces, she said the only jigsaws they kept now were for children, that there was little demand for the more difficult ones anymore, then asked if she might help him find something else. Furlong shook his head but bought a bag of the Lemon's jellies hanging on one of the hooks behind her head, as he did not like to go back out with one arm as long as the other.

At Joyce's Furniture, he caught his reflection in a full-length mirror that was for sale and decided he should go on to the barber's, for a haircut. When he looked in, there was a long queue but he pushed the door and at once a little bell tinkled. He took his place at the end of the bench to wait his turn beside a red-haired man he did not know and four red-haired boys who much resembled him. Sinnott, with one too many taken, was in the chair with the barber standing over him finishing a short back and sides. The barber nodded solemnly at Furlong in the mirror and carried on with the shears for a while before putting the shears down and brushing the hairs off the back of Sinnott's neck, and emptying out the ashtray. When the butts landed in the bucket, some hair singed a little, giving out a bitter smell, and Furlong thought over what Eileen had been told about the barber's son, the young electrician, of his diagnosis, and how the lad had been given little time. Some talk rose up then, between the men, and a few rough jokes were bandied, in disguise, on account of there being children there.

Furlong found himself not joining in the talk so much as keeping it at bay while thinking over and imagining other things. At one point, after more customers had come in and Furlong had shifted across the bench, before the mirror, he looked directly at his reflection, searching for a resemblance to Ned, which he both could and could not see. Maybe the woman out at Wilson's had been mistaken and had simply imagined the likeness, assuming they were kin. But this did not seem likely and he could not help thinking over how down-hearted Ned had been in himself after Furlong's mother had passed away, and how they had always gone to Mass and eaten together, the way they stayed up talking at the fire at night, what sense it made. And if this was truth, hadn't it been an act of daily grace, on Ned's part, to make Furlong believe that he had come from finer stock, while watching steadfastly over him, through the years. This was the man who had polished his shoes and tied the laces, who'd bought him his first razor and taught him how to shave. Why were the things that were closest so often the hardest to see?

His mind was freeing up now, given pause to stray and roam, and he couldn't say that he at all minded sitting there, waiting his turn with the year's work over for him – and by the time his hair was cut and the cut was paid for and he stepped out, the snow was building so that the footprints of people who had gone before and after him in both directions stood out plainly and not so plainly, too, on the footpath.

In Charles Street, he stopped at Hanrahan's to collect the patent leather shoes he'd ordered for Eileen, which had been set aside. The well-dressed woman behind the counter, the wife of one of his good customers, didn't seem overly eager to serve him, but she brought out the box of shoes.

'It was the sixes you wanted?'

'Sixes,' Furlong said. 'Aye.'

'Would you like them wrapped?'

She was putting them side by side, folding the tissue paper over, and closing the lid on the box.

'Aye,' Furlong said. 'If you wouldn't mind.'

He watched her wrapping it, pulling the sellotape from the reel and creasing the corners of the holly-patterned paper before sliding the box into a plastic bag and telling him how much he owed.

When Furlong paid and went out, it was well past dark and he was more than ready to climb the hill towards home, but he caught the smell of hot oil from the chipper's, whose door had opened, and stopped in to buy a can of 7UP which he drank thirstily at the counter before he found himself walking back down to the river and on towards the bridge, where a surge of cold and tiredness passed through him. The snow was still coming down, although timidly, dropping from the sky on all that was there, and he wondered why he had not gone back to the comforts and safety of his own home – Eileen would already be preparing for midnight Mass and would be wondering where he was – but his day was filling up now, with something else.

Crossing the bridge, he looked down at the

river, at the water flowing past. People said that a curse had been placed on the Barrow. Furlong couldn't remember the half of it but it had to do with an order of monks who'd built an abbey there, in the old days, and were given the right to levy tolls on the river. As time went on, they grew covetous and the people had rebelled and driven them from the town. When they were leaving, the abbot put a curse on the town, so that every year it would take three lives, neither more nor fewer. His mother herself had believed there was some truth in it, had told him of a cattle-dealer she'd known whose lorry had gone off the road one New Year's Eve and how he'd lost his life, the third drowning that year. She used to sometimes hold him in her strong, freckled arm while she turned the handle of the churn with the other; used to lay her head against the cow's side and sing a song or two while she was milking with Ned in the evenings, to ease the milk coming down. And she had slapped him too, sometimes, for being bold or talking out of turn or leaving the lid off the butter-dish, but those things were only small.

Furlong carried on uneasily, thinking back over the Dublin girl who'd asked him to take her here so she could drown, and how he had refused her; of how he had afterwards lost his way along the back roads, and of the queer old man out slashing the thistles in the fog that evening with the puckaun, and what he'd said about how the road would take him wherever he wanted to go.

When he reached the far bank of the river, he walked on, up the hill, passing other types of houses with lighted candles and handsome, red poinsettias in the front rooms, houses he'd never before looked into, only from outside the back door. In one, a young boy, wearing a blazer, was seated at a piano while a beautifully dressed woman, holding a long-stemmed glass, stood at his side, listening. In another house, a worried-looking man was bent over a desk, writing things down as though he was making difficult calculations, trying to balance the books. In yet another, a small boy on a rocking horse was riding across a deep, wool rug. A girl in a St Margaret's uniform was seated on a velvet settee, and Furlong wondered over her wearing it outside of schooldays but maybe she had come from choir practice.

On he walked, up the hill, past the reach of the lighted houses and the streetlights. In the dark and quiet he there took a turn around the outside of the convent, taking stock of the place. The huge, high walls all around the back were also topped with broken glass, still visible, at points, under the snow. It was not possible to see in, and the third-storey windows were blackened over and fitted with metal grilles. He went on feeling not unlike a nocturnal animal on the prowl and hunting, with a current of something close to excitement running through his blood. Turning a corner, he came across a black cat eating from the carcass of a crow, licking her lips. On seeing him, she froze, then fled through the hedge.

When he walked back round to the main entrance, past the open gates and on up the drive-way, the yews and evergreens were pretty as a picture, just as people had said, with berries on the holly bushes. There was but one set of footprints in the snow, heading faintly in the opposite direction, and he reached and easily passed the front door without meeting anyone. When he got to the gable and went round to the coal-house door, the need to open it left him, queerly, before it just as soon came back, and then he slid the bolt across and called her name and gave his own. He'd imagined, while he was in the barber's, that the door might now be locked or that she, blessedly, might not be within or that he might have had to carry her for part of the way and wondered how he'd manage, if he did, or what he'd do, or if he'd do anything at all, or if he'd even come here – but everything was just as he'd feared although the girl, this time, took his coat and seemed gladly to lean on him as he led her out.

'You'll come home with me now, Sarah.'

Easily enough he helped her along the front drive and down the hill, past the fancy houses and on towards the bridge. Crossing the river, his eyes again fell on the stout-black water flowing darkly along – and a part of him envied the Barrow's knowledge of her course, how easily the water followed its incorrigible way, so freely to the open sea. The air was sharper now, without his coat, and he felt his self-preservation and courage battling against each other and thought, once more, of taking the girl to the priest's house – but several times, already, his mind had gone on ahead, and met him there, and had concluded that the priests already knew. Sure hadn't Mrs Kehoe as much as told him so?

They're all the one.

As they walked on, Furlong met people he had known and dealt with for the greater part of his life, most of whom gladly stopped to speak until, looking down, they saw the bare, black feet and realised the girl with him was not one of his own. Some then gave them a wide berth or talked awkwardly or politely wished him a Happy Christmas and went on. One elderly woman out walking a terrier on a long strap confronted him, asking who the girl was, and was she not one of those wans from the laundry? At another point, a little boy looked at Sarah's feet and laughed and called her dirty before his father gave his hand a rough tug and told him to whisht. Miss Kenny, wearing old clothes he'd never before seen her in and with drink on her breath, stopped and asked what he was doing with a child out in the snow with no shoes on, assuming Sarah was one of his own, and marched off. Not one person they met addressed Sarah or asked where he was taking her. Feeling little or no obligation to say very much or to explain, Furlong smoothed things over as best he could and carried on along with the excitement in his heart matched by the fear of what he could not yet see but knew he would encounter.

As they were nearing the centre of town and the Christmas lights, a part of him considered backing off and taking the long way home but he braved it out and carried on, following the path he ordinarily would have taken. A change, it seemed, was coming over the girl and soon she had to stop, and vomited on the street.

'Good girl,' Furlong encouraged her. 'Get it all up. Get that much out of you.'

In the Square, she paused to rest at the lighted manger and stood in a type of trance, looking in. Furlong looked in, too; at Joseph's bright robes, the kneeling Virgin, the sheep. Someone, since last he'd seen it, had placed the figures of the wise men and the Baby Jesus there but it was the donkey that held the girl's attention, and she reached out to stroke and push the snow off his ear.

'Isn't he lovely,' she said.

'We've not far to go now,' Furlong assured. 'We're almost home.'

As they carried on along and met more people Furlong did and did not know, he found himself asking was there any point in being alive without helping one another? Was it possible to carry on along through all the years, the decades, through an entire life, without once being brave enough to go against what was there and yet call yourself a Christian, and face yourself in the mirror?

How light and tall he almost felt walking along with this girl at his side and some fresh, new, unrecognisable joy in his heart. Was it possible that the best bit of him was shining forth, and surfacing? Some part of him, whatever it could be called – was there any name for it? – was going wild, he knew. The fact was that he would pay for it but never once in his whole and unremarkable life had he known a happiness akin to this, not even when his infant girls were first placed in his arms and he had heard their healthy, obstinate cries.

He thought of Mrs Wilson, of her daily kindnesses, of how she had corrected and encouraged him, of the small things she had said and done and had refused to do and say and what she must have known, the things which, when added up, amounted to a life. Had it not been for her, his mother might very well have wound up in that place. In an earlier time, it could have been his own mother he was saving – if saving was what this could be called. And only God knew what would have happened to him, where he might have ended up.

The worst was yet to come, he knew. Already he could feel a world of trouble waiting for him behind the next door, but the worst that could have happened was also already behind him; the thing not done, which could have been – which he would have had to live with for the rest of his life. Whatever suffering he was now to meet was a long way from what the girl at his side had already endured, and might yet surpass. Climbing the street towards his own front door with the barefooted girl and the box of shoes, his fear more than outweighed every other feeling but in his foolish heart he not only hoped but legitimately believed that they would manage.

A Note on the Text

This is a work of fiction based in no part on any individual or individuals. Ireland's last Magdalen laundry was not closed down until 1996. It is not known how many girls and women were concealed, incarcerated and forced to labour in these institutions. Ten thousand is the modest figure; thirty thousand is probably more accurate. Most of the records from the Magdalen laundries were destroyed, lost, or made inaccessible. Rarely was any of these girls' or women's work recognised or acknowledged in any way. Many girls and women lost their babies. Some lost their lives. Some or most lost the lives they could have had. It is not known how many thousands of infants died in these institutions or were adopted out from the mother-and-baby homes. Earlier this year, the Mother and Baby Home Commission Report found that nine thousand children died in just eighteen of the institutions investigated. In 2014, the historian Catherine Corless made public her shocking discovery that 796 babies died between 1925 and 1961 in the Tuam home, in County Galway. These institutions were run and financed by the Catholic Church in concert with the Irish State. No apology was issued by the Irish government over the Magdalen laundries until Taoiseach Enda Kenny did so in 2013.

Acknowledgements

The author wishes to express her thanks to Aosdána and The Arts Council, Wexford County Council, The Authors' Foundation, The Heinrich Böll Association and to Trinity College, Dublin, for their support.

Thanks also to Kathryn Baird, Felicity Blunt, Alex Bowler, Tina Callaghan, Mary Clayton, Ian Critchley, Ita Daly, Dr Noreen Doody, Grainne Doran, Morgan Entrekin, Liam Halpin, Margaret Huntington, Claire and Jim Keegan, Sally Keogh, Loretta Kinsella, Ita Lennon, Niall MacMonagle, Michael McCarthy, Patricia McCarthy, Mary McCay, Helen McGoldrick, Eoin McNamee, James Meaney, Sophia Ní Sheoin, Claire Nozieres, Jacqueline Odin, Stephen Page, Rosie Pierce, Sheila Purdy, Katie Raissian, Josephine Salverda, Claire Simpson, Jennifer Smith, Anna Stein, Dervla Tierney and Sabine Wespieser.

And to my students who have taught me so much over the years.